LEARN TO BE KIND

FOREST FRIENDS LEARN TO BE KIND
Text copyright © 1993 by Danae Dobson.
Illustrations copyright © 1993 by Cuitlahuac Morales.

Managing Editor: Laura Minchew
Project Editor: Beverly Phillips

Library of Congress Cataloging-in-Publication Data

Dobson, Danae.
    Forest friends learn to be kind / Danae Dobson ; illustrated by
Cuitlahuac Morales.
        p.   cm. — Forest friends series
    "Word kids!"
    Summary: In a dream, six-year-old Eric helps his forest animal
friends understand that in assuming Geronimo the bear is dangerous
they have misjudged him.
    ISBN 0-8499-1016-1
    [1. Forest animals—Fiction. 2. Dreams—Fiction. 3. Conduct of life—Fiction.]
I. Morales, Cuitlahuac, 1967–   ill. II. Title.
III. Series: Dobson, Danae. Forest friends series.
PZ7.D6614For 1993
[E]—dc20
                                                                    93-10794
                                                                    CIP
                                                                    AC

Printed in the United States of America
3 4 5 6 7 8 9 LBM 9 8 7 6 5 4 3 2 1

FOREST FRIENDS

LEARN TO BE KIND

DANAE DOBSON

Illustrated by Cuitlahuac Morales

WORD
Kids!

WORD PUBLISHING

Dallas•London•Vancouver•Melbourne

"See you tomorrow," said Mother, handing her son a sleeping bag. "Have a good time!"

Eric Martin hurried to the house next door and rang the doorbell. Pretty soon his friend, Tommy Merino, came to greet him.

"Hi!" said Tommy. "I'm glad you're here!"

Eric was excited. Tommy's dad owned a camping tent. And tonight the two boys were going to sleep outside in it!

"Come on," called Tommy. "Let's go look at the tent!"

Eric followed his friend to the backyard.

"Wow!" said Eric. "It's so big!"

"Yeah, and it's a real one, too! Not like one of those plastic toys!"

Just then, Mrs. Merino called them inside for supper.

After they had eaten, she helped them carry their things to the tent.

"Now remember, Tommy," said Mrs. Merino, "you can only sleep here until your father and I go to bed. It might not be safe to stay outside all night."

"Okay," said Tommy as he gave his mother a kiss. "Good night!"

The two boys snuggled into their sleeping bags.

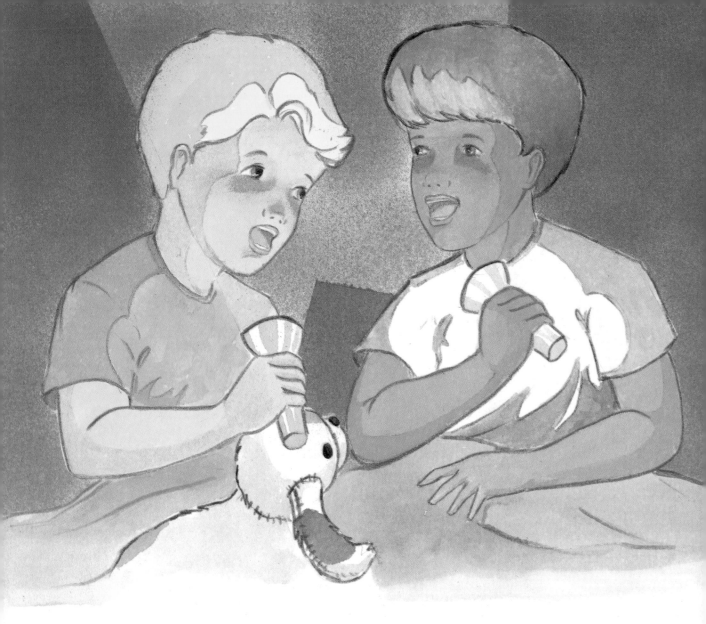

Eric had brought his favorite stuffed dog, Tucker. He held Tucker close as Tommy turned off the flashlight.

Suddenly, they heard a loud noise!

"What was that?" asked Eric.

"Don't worry. It's just an owl," said Tommy. "Hey, do you know any scary stories?"

Eric thought for a moment. "No," he said. "Do you?"

"I know lots of them!" said Tommy.

Eric listened as Tommy told one story after another.
But they didn't sound very scary to Eric. Before long, Eric
started to yawn. Tommy was still talking as his friend
drifted to sleep.

Soon, Eric began to have a dream. He was in a place he had been before. It was called Big Green Forest. Eric often dreamed about his animal friends who lived there. Something exciting was always happening in Big Green Forest!

Eric set Tucker on the grass and looked around.

The little dog began to growl. "What is it, Tucker?" asked the boy. "What's the matter?"

Just then, Eric saw his friend Fawna the Deer running toward them.

"Eric!" she called. "Quickly—follow me!"

"What's wrong?" asked Eric.

"I'll explain later," said the deer. "Right now we have to hurry!" Fawna led Eric and Tucker through the woods. Before long, they arrived at Mrs. Rabbit's house.

When Eric came through the door, he was surprised to see all his friends. There was Oliver the Skunk, Woodrow the Beaver, and Sidney the Squirrel. Over in the corner sat Mrs. Rabbit with her twins, Pinky and Pookie.

Eric's friends looked very worried.

"Will someone please tell me what's going on?" he asked.

"There is danger in Big Green Forest," Fawna said. "Geronimo is back!"

"Geronimo?" asked Eric. "Who is that?"

"He's a big, mean bear!" said Pookie. "He lives in a cave high in the mountains. Sometimes he comes to our forest looking for food."

"And we have to hide until he goes away," added Pinky.

"That's terrible!" said Eric. "But how do you know he's coming *now*?"

"Fawna saw him and warned all of us," said Sidney.

Suddenly, a loud noise shook the forest!
"Here he comes!" shouted Woodrow. "Everybody push against the front door!"

Eric and the animals leaned against the door. Their hearts were pounding! Fawna stayed by the window to watch for Geronimo. They could hear the bear's paws thundering across the ground. The noise was so loud even the dishes in the cabinet were rattling!

Just then, Fawna spotted Geronimo in the distance! He was headed straight toward Mrs. Rabbit's house!

"Oh, no!" said Fawna. "Here he comes!"
Quickly, she joined the others as they pushed against the door with all their might.

The pounding of the bear's paws grew louder and louder. Before long, Geronimo was just outside the door!
"Push, everyone! Push hard!" Eric shouted.

Suddenly the sound stopped! Eric held his breath.
"Where did he go?" asked Fawna.

"I don't know," said Eric. "But we need to stay here until it's safe." The boy and his friends waited a long time. They could hear nothing.

Finally, Fawna walked back to the window to look for the bear. She gasped in terror! Geronimo was staring right at her through the glass!

Fawna was just about to scream when she noticed something strange—the bear was smiling! In fact, he looked downright friendly!

Fawna called Eric and the others to the window.
"I don't believe it!" said Woodrow. "Maybe he's not mean at all!"
"Let's go outside and say hello," said Oliver.
"No, it's not safe!" said Sidney. "I've heard that Geronimo eats little animals for breakfast!"

"Well, he doesn't look dangerous to me," said Oliver. "I'm going to open the door!"

"No! No!" said Eric. "You can't do that. What if he is mean? None of us will be safe!"

"Just watch!" said Oliver.

With that, he swung open the door to the house.

Everyone gasped and ran to the back of the room. But Geronimo just sat outside, smiling and looking at the other animals.

"Hi!" said Oliver. "Would you like to be our . . . friend?"
The bear looked happy as he nodded his head.

After waiting a few minutes, Eric and the animals came outside to meet him.

"Wow!" said Pookie. "A real bear! A real *friendly* bear!"

"He's a *big* one, too!" added Pinky.

"Would you like something to eat?" asked Mrs. Rabbit.

Once again, Geronimo nodded his head.

"I don't think he talks," said Pookie. "But he sure isn't mean like everyone thought! He's just a lonely old bear looking for friends!"

"I remember my Sunday school teacher told me it is wrong to think badly about people," said Eric. "All of us were judging Geronimo before he did anything wrong. I think we all learned something today."

Eric turned and looked at Geronimo. The bear was busy eating the honey and berries Mrs. Rabbit had given him. After he finished the food, he played with Eric and the animals. He even gave Pinky and Pookie rides on his back! Everyone had indeed made a new friend!

After a while Eric heard someone calling his name. He knew that once again it was time to leave Big Green Forest.

"Good-bye, Geronimo!" said Eric. "Thanks for being my friend!"

The animals waved as Eric and Tucker headed into the woods.

Eric slowly opened his eyes. Mrs. Merino was leaning over him, saying it was time to come in the house. Eric yawned as he and Tommy picked up their sleeping bags. The two boys followed Mrs. Merino across the backyard.

"It was fun sleeping in the tent," said Eric. "Can we do it again sometime?"

"Sure!" said Tommy. "Maybe next weekend!"

"Do you remember when I said I didn't know any scary stories?" asked Eric. "Well, I have a *good* one now!"

"You do?" asked Tommy. "What is it?"

Eric gave Tucker a little squeeze against his chest.
"Well, once upon a time there was this mean ol' bear named Geronimo . . ."